Ghostly Holler-Day

Daren King studied in Bath and lives in London. *Mouse Noses on Toast*, his first book for children, won the Gold Nestlé Children's Prize. *Peter the Penguin Pioneer* was shortlisted for the Blue Peter Award. He is the author of four adult books. *Boxy an Star* was shortlisted for the *Guardian* First Book Award.

David Roberts is the award-winning illustrator of over 30 titles. He has had a variety of interesting jobs, such as hair washer, shelf stacker, egg fryer and hat designer. He was born in Liverpool and now lives in London.

Praise for Daren King:

'Children will laugh out loud at the zany humour and the witty one-liners . . . while David Roberts' comical illustrations can't fail to raise a giggle.' *Scholastic Literacy Time Plus Magazine*

'King is very good at making children think about their world . . . hugely inventive and charmingly funny, early readers will adore having this book read to them and will love trying it themselves.' *Literary Review*

'Writer and illustrator have produced an hilarious fun-packed riot.' *Herald*

Ghostly Holler-Day

Daren King
Illustrations by David Roberts

Quercus

First published in Great Britain in 2010 by

Quercus
21 Bloomsbury Square
London
WC1A 2NS

A CIP catalogue reference for this book is available
from the British Library

ISBN 978 1 85738 045 6

Printed and bound in Great Britain by Clays Ltd, St Ives plc.

For Rebecca

Also by this author

MOUSE NOSES ON TOAST
SENSIBLE HARE AND THE CASE OF CARROTS
PETER THE PENGUIN PIONEER
FRIGHTFULLY FRIENDLY GHOSTIES

Contents

1

The Postcard

If you had seen us ghosties gathered on the front lawn that morning, winter coats buttoned up to our glum faces, you'd have thought we were on our way to a funeral.

But then you'd have noticed the suitcases with Agatha's hat box on top like a cherry on a cake, and the penny would've dropped. Those ghosties are off on their holler-days.

I'm Charlie, by the way. Charlie Vapour. I take my hat off to you!

It all started yesterday evening, with Wither

hiding the postcard from Headless Leslie.

No, let me think—

It started with us lot floating about in the hall, bored out of our haunted heads. Tabitha had an idea, and the light bulb popped. That always happens when Tabitha has an idea.

Tabitha Tumbly is a poltergeist, see, and that means she can move things and make things happen, using the power of thought.

2

One minute you're wisping about in the glare of the chandelier or that antique lamp by the bookcase, and the next thing you know, Tabitha has one of her bright ideas and the room is plunged into darkness. And there's Pamela Fraidy trembling with fright and Wither blubbing about the price of light bulbs.

'What us ghosties need,' said Tabitha as we flitted about in the darkness, 'is a holler-day.'

'A holler-day?' I said. 'You mean, the sort you go on, then come back?'

'It usually works like that,' Tabitha said. 'A holler-day, by the sea.'

We all wisped into the light of the lounge.

'That is a super idea,' Agatha said, clutching her pearls. 'Every ghosty loves a holler-day.'

'And it's dead boring around here,' Humphrey Bump said, 'since the still-alives moved out.'

'But it's winter,' said Wither, gazing through

the lounge window at the blue-black sky. 'My knees will knock.'

'The sun always shines by the sea,' I told the daft old fool. 'At least, that's how I remember it, from when I was a boy.'

Agatha Draft floated over to the coffee table and grabbed a couple of holler-day brochures. 'Frighten-on-Sea, or Scare-borough?'

The trouble was, me, Pamela and Agatha fancied Scare-borough, and the other three favoured Frighten.

That was when we caught Wither hiding something behind the carriage clock on the mantelpiece. 'What have you got there?' I asked him, and he turned red – well, as red as you can get when you've been dead two hundred years – and wisped behind the clock.

'Why did he wisp behind the clock?' Humphrey asked me, loosening his school tie.

'He's embarrassed,' I told the boy. 'Wither

4

always wisps behind the clock when he's been caught doing something he shouldn't.'

It took us ten minutes to get Wither out from behind that clock. We tried everything.

Humphrey Bump bumped the clock with his fat

5

belly, and Tabitha jiggled the clock this way and that. I crossed my fingers behind my back and told Wither that if he came out, we'd let him perform one of his poems.

'Aggie,' Tabitha said, turning to Agatha Draft, 'you could rustle up one of your force ten gales, and blow him out.'

'I would,' Agatha said, 'if I had I the skills.'

'Rubbish,' I told her. 'If there's any ghosty who can blow Wither out from behind that carriage clock, it's you, Aggie.'

Agatha Draft possesses the ghostly ability to create an eerie breeze at will – the sort of breeze that ruffles a gentleman's collar, and makes the cat's fur stand on end.

'Look away, then,' Agatha said, and we all turned to the window while Agatha sent the clock sailing along the mantelpiece.

When Wither tumbled out, looking flustered and mixed up, he was holding this seaside

6

postcard. GREETINGS FROM FRIGHTEN, it said on the front.

Humphrey snatched the postcard from Wither's bony, boneless fingers, blew a raspberry and handed the postcard to Tabitha.

'It's from Headless Leslie,' said Tabitha. 'Wither, this postcard is addressed to all of us. Why did you hide it behind the clock?'

The stubborn old fool refused to answer. He just floated by the fireplace with his hands in his trouser pockets, then wrinkled his brow in thought and said, 'Charlie, you told me that if I floated out from behind the clock, you would allow me to recite one of my poems. Well, here I am, and—'

'You didn't float out,' I said. 'Agatha had to blow you out.'

Tabitha handed Wither the postcard. 'You can read out Leslie's postcard instead.'

Wither floated over to the chandelier, and

7

tried to make out Leslie's spidery handwriting. He cleared his throat and started reading in that warbly, passionate voice he puts on when he recites poetry.

Humphrey stuffed his fingers in his ears and poked his tongue out.

'Normal voice, please,' Tabitha said. 'We can't make out a word you're saying.'

Leslie had written about how he'd gone on holler-day to Frighten, and how he had forgotten the way back.

'No wonder we haven't seen him since August,' Tabitha said.

'Headless Leslie would forget his head if it wasn't screwed on,' said Pamela.

'It isn't,' said Wither.

'But he wrote the address on the postcard,' I said, straightening my trilby hat. 'If he hadn't, it'd never have got here.'

'He must have forgotten the address after he

wrote it down,' Tabitha said. 'And perhaps he then tried to read it, but couldn't read the handwriting.'

'Leslie's handwriting is frightfully spidery,' said Pamela Fraidy, and she shivered.

Agatha floated about the lounge, rattling her pearls and fluttering her elegant eyelashes. 'Our decision has been made for us. We holler-day in Frighten, and find our dear friend Headless Leslie.'

'And his head,' said Wither. 'Don't forget his head.'

2
Wartime Ticket Office

So that's how it came about. A haunted
holler-day by the sea, in the dead of winter.

Trouble was, we had to get there first, and we
had an awful lot of luggage. And Humphrey
Bump had this rubber ring around his waist –
'Just think of all the bumping you can do with
that,' Agatha said – and he'd inflated it so big
he could hardly fit through the front door.

Not only that, but us ghosties aren't terribly
popular. Odd, really. After all, we're frightfully
friendly.

11

It was too cold to be outside if you didn't have to, so there weren't a lot of villagers about. The only still-alive we passed was the batty old woman from down the road, who shook her walking stick at Pamela Fraidy and yelled something mean.

Poor Pamela. She's a nervous wreck as it is, and that old woman is enough to give anyone the shivers.

The moment we floated into the village train station, dragging our ghostly luggage, the ticket office door slammed shut and a CLOSED sign flapped into place behind the glass.

'This always happens when we try to buy train tickets,' said Wither, glancing at his pocket watch. 'Our sense of timing is atrocious.'

'There's always the old wartime ticket office,' I said with a wink.

'That ticket office was destroyed during the Blitz,' said Tabitha. 'I wasn't born back then, but my grandfather told me all about it.'

'Bombed out or not,' I said, 'it's still open, for those in the know.'

We flitted further down the track to where the train station used to be, and the air shimmered as the wartime ticket office materialised before our eyes.

There was a big hole in the roof and the windows had shattered, and there was a good deal of smoke, and when the station master floated out from under the counter he had his fingers in his ears, and his spectacles were speckled with dust and soot.

'Six terrifying tickets,' I told the man, doffing my hat.

'This ticket office is spiffing,' Agatha said. 'Is there a ghostly wartime train, too?'

'There is,' I said, 'but it's a steam train, so it's a bit on the slow side, if you know what I mean.'

13

'Trains should go super fast,' Humphrey said, bumping this way and that.

'The still-alives will make room for us on the still-alive train,' Tabitha said. 'They always do.'

'Only because they don't want to sit with us,' said Wither. 'You know how mean-spirited they are.'

3

Frighten-on-Sea

As we unloaded our luggage at Frighten
Station, Pamela trembled with cold, Wither's
teeth chattered and Agatha sneezed an eerie,
breezy sneeze. I had to pull my hat right down
to my pencil-thin moustache to keep the wind
out of my eyeballs.

'Where is everybody?' said Pamela. There
were no still-alives on the platform, and most of
the passengers had left the train at Ghoole.

'It's November,' Pamela said. 'Who visits the
seaside in winter?'

'A lot of people live in Frighten,' Tabitha said.

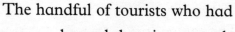

The handful of tourists who had braved the winter weather screamed at us and ran off, which ain't exactly friendly, you have to admit.

'This place is like a ghost town,' said Wither as we floated onto the main street.

'I expect they're all on the beach,' Agatha said. 'Winter it may be, but us ghosties are on our holler-days, and I intend to make the most of it.' She lifted the lid from her hat box and placed an elegant floppy sunhat on her head.

'My arms are tired,' said Pamela Fraidy. 'Charlie, Wither, sorry to be a frightful bore, but if you two ghosties were gentlemen you would offer to carry our cases.'

'Yes, of course,' I said, sort of polite but

18

miffed at the same time.

The three girl-ghosties dropped their luggage and skipped off into the chilly air.

'I'm too old and angular for luggage,' Wither said, flexing his bony arms. 'Charlie, you and Humphrey can carry it. I'm a poet, not a carthorse. I'd put my back out, and—'

'And I'm too dapper,' I said, adjusting my cufflinks. 'Humphrey's good at carrying luggage.' Before Humphrey could protest, I loaded him up with the six ghostly suitcases, Agatha's hat box and Pamela's bucket and spade.

'Tabitha, you must be frightfully cold in that bikini,' Pamela said.

'Not at all,' Tabitha said, rubbing her goose-pimply arms.

'The sea air is bracing,'

19

Agatha gasped as we turned onto the promenade. 'And – oh – I do believe it has stolen my hat.'

A winter gale had blown in from across the sea, tossing the waves this way and that, whistling through Wither's bony head, in one ear and out the other, and the wind had snatched Agatha's floppy sunhat and wisped it away.

I had to laugh. Well, she did look a sight, chasing after it down the prom-tiddly-om-pom-pom. And of course, Agatha being the breezy sort, she couldn't help but rustle up a breeze of her own. The closer she got to the sunhat the further along the promenade it blew.

'Don't just float there,' Agatha yelled. 'Float over here and help.'

The sunhat didn't stop tossing and tumbling until it walloped into a tatty old newsstand, situated on the edge of the beach. Agatha retrieved it from a pile of crumpled newspapers and blew dust from the floppy brim.

As Tabitha, Wither, Pamela and myself floated over, a group of tourists flung their buckets and spades into the air and ran off down the street.

'Why are you all leaving?' Wither asked them. 'Is it something we said?'

'Ghosts!' one of the tourists screamed back as they disappeared out of sight.

'I think they may be right,' Tabitha whispered into my ear. She was studying the headlines on the newsstand. 'It seems Frighten-on-Sea is haunted.'

FRIGHTEN PIER HAUNTED BY HEADLESS GHOST, the headline read.

'Don't tell poor Pamela,' said Agatha, arranging her sunhat. 'Ghosts terrify her, and she's a nervous wreck as it is.'

'Don't tell me what?' Pamela Fraidy said

with eyes like teacups.

It was myself, Charlie Vapour esquire – I take my hat off to you – who pointed out the obvious. 'The headless ghost is our Leslie.'

'Headless Leslie wouldn't haunt,' said Agatha. 'He may have been dead since Elizabethan times, but he's frightfully sweet, and it's hardly his fault his head comes off.'

A hackney carriage pulled up, led by a transparent horse. It was the sort of transport they'd have had in Frighten before I was born, back in Wither's time. The roof was loaded up with luggage. Humphrey Bump sat perched at the very top, stuffing his big round head with doughnuts.

'The hotel on Starfish Street,' I told the driver as I sat with the girls in the carriage. I closed the door and fastened the ghostly latch.

'This is frightfully fun,' Agatha said as the carriage lurched forward. 'I say, where's Wither?'

'Hither,' said Wither, and in through the window he wisped.

4
The Caped Figure

All that talk of hauntings gave me the shivers. I couldn't sleep that night, and after an hour of tossing and turning I decided to float out for a lungful of fresh air.

At least, that was what I told Wither.

The daft old fool was snoring his head off in the top bunk – Humphrey tends to go bump in the night, so we gave him a double bed to himself in the next room, and the girls shared a room across the hall – but of course, the moment my big toe touched the carpet he woke up.

Truth is, I had a spot of business to attend to. Wink-wink, nudge-nudge, say no more.

I floated into my comfy slippers, tied the cord of my dressing gown, then wisped under the bedroom door and down the dimly lit hallway to the back of the hotel, where I passed through the outer wall.

That's this little trick of mine.

Every ghosty has a ghostly skill, as I've said. There's Wither's ability to write the most dreadful poetry, and Humphrey's ability to bump into everything in sight, for example.

Well, I'm the only ghosty with the talent to pass through walls, ceilings and floors, even when wearing a hat.

Though I have to say, normally I remove the trilby when I pass through. After all, it is the polite thing to do. But what with this cold weather –

Anyway, so there I am out in this alleyway in

my pyjamas, the trilby warming my bald patch, when who should float out of the shadows but my old mate Alfie Spectre.

I've known Alfie since I was a small boy. He lives just down the road there, about a minute's float from this very hotel. At least, he did when he was still alive.

'Hello, Alfie,' I said, doffing my trilby. 'Fancy meeting you here.'

'Hello, Charlie,' Alfie said with a smirk.

The minute we'd decided to holler-day in Frighten, I'd called Alfie on the phantom phone, told him we should meet for a spot of business.

That's how I make my living, if you pardon the pun. I buy and sell whatever I can lay my haunted hands on.

'What have you got for me this cold winter's night?' I said.

Alfie unfastened his buttons and there they were, half a dozen gold watches pinned to the lining of his army coat.

'Are they hot, Alfie?' I said. That's a cockney way of asking if the watches were stolen.

Now, don't get me wrong, I'm no angel – that's a trilby on my head, not a halo – but I don't buy stolen goods. I'm a gentleman, see?

'Nothing's hot in this weather,' Alfie said with a wink.

'That's good enough for me,' I said, and I bought all six.

But something was wrong.

When Alfie counted those pound notes and tucked them into his pocket, his hands were trembling like he'd seen a, um, ghost.

Alfie had been a soldier, he'd been killed in the trenches, that's why I'm in my forties and poor Alfie is still only twenty-one. He was a brave lad, our Alfie, and it took a lot to make his hands shake.

'Alfie, whatever is the matter?'

'Do you have far to float home, Charlie?'

I glanced at the brickwork to my left, and gave Alfie a wink. 'A pass-through, a wisp and a float, and I'll be tucked up in no time.'

'I'd get going, if I were you,' Alfie said. 'There's a lot of funny people about.'

'How do you mean?'

Alfie lowered his voice. 'Charlie, there's been – shall we say, sightings.'

This made me laugh so hard I almost dropped my hat. 'That'll be my old mate Headless Leslie. He wisped down to Frighten for his summer holler-days and forgot the way home.'

29

Alfie frowned. It was hard to tell in the glow of the streetlamp, but his face looked white. 'I've met your mate Leslie, and this wasn't him. This chap was a good deal more sinister than your mate Leslie.'

'Rubbish,' I said, and I tried to do that thing where you flick the rim of your trilby with your finger and it does a somersault and you catch it on your elbow.

Trouble was, Alfie had got me nervous, and I poked out the wrong elbow and missed my target. The trilby tumbled into the darkness.

As I lifted the trilby from a frosty puddle I heard this muffled yell, and when I wisped back up Alfie had gone.

It ain't like Alfie to float off without saying goodbye. He's playing a prank on me, I told myself as I tightened the cord of my dressing gown. A regular joker, is our Alfie. He'll be hiding behind a wall, I thought, ready to wisp

out and yell BOO.

That was when this creepy feeling came over me, like I was being watched.

When I turned around, there it was. A figure dressed in black, a top hat on its head, two red eyes peering out from behind this flowing purple cape.

So now I knew why Alfie Spectre had wisped off.

I didn't stop to find out where he'd got to. I passed through that wall as quick as my transparent bits would float me, and wisped off to bed.

5

The Fortune Teller

'You look terrible,' Tabitha said when we gathered on the beach the following afternoon.

'Wither snores,' I said.

All right, so that weren't the real reason I hadn't slept. The truth is, after seeing that caped figure in the alleyway I'd spent the rest of the night staring into the darkness.

I kept thinking I should tell the other ghosties about what I'd seen, but I didn't want to spoil the holler-day.

Agatha floated down the sandy wooden steps that led up onto the pier. 'The pier is

33

closed,' she said, fiddling with the brim of her floppy sunhat. 'Some holler-day this has turned out to be. I told you we should have gone to Scare-borough.'

'We can always find a way to amuse ourselves,' said Tabitha. 'Perhaps some of these amusement machines are switched on.'

'You could make them work,' said Pamela, 'using your poltergeist skills.'

'I'm afraid my poltergeist skills just aren't that powerful,' Tabitha said. 'I can make a policeman's helmet topple from his head, or a cyclist cycle backwards, but electricity is something else.'

'I want candyfloss,' Humphrey said, bumping into a brightly painted candyfloss machine.

'If Humphrey doesn't get his candyfloss,' Agatha said, 'we'll never hear the end of it.'

'Hide your eyes then,' said Tabitha. 'I'm awfully shy, you know.'

Me, Humphrey and Pamela covered our eyes with our hands, and Agatha hid behind her floppy sunhat.

It's not the polite thing to do, I know, but I couldn't help peeking. Well, I bet the other ghosties did the same.

The turny thing turned and the whizzy bit whizzed, and this big tuft of pink candyfloss oozed through a tube and into a plastic bag, which popped out through an opening in the bottom of the machine. Humphrey grabbed it with a greedy hand and licked his lips.

It was at that moment that I spotted this stripy tent thing on the edge of the beach. 'There is one attraction still open,' I said. 'Look.'

A wooden sign at the entrance read FORTUNE TELLER. We all wisped in through the open flap, and I paid the fortune teller 50p.

The old woman fixed me with her eerie gaze,

rubbed this crystal ball with her hands, and started to spout drivel about our future.

'Ye shall find what ye seek on the pier,' the old woman moaned, and when she nodded her head her hoop earrings jiggled. 'Even though it is closed for the duration,' she added. 'Seek, and ye shall find.'

36

'She means Headless Leslie,' Agatha whispered.

'And you, miss,' the fortune teller groaned, staring into Agatha's eyes, 'will breeze about in a floppy sunhat, and you, boy,' she wailed, turning to Humphrey, 'will bump into things and annoy the seagulls.'

'What a frightfully accurate reading,' Agatha blushed.

'It's almost like she's one of us,' I said.

'Funny you should say that, Charlie,' Pamela said, 'but the fortune teller looks like Wither.'

'I say,' said Tabitha, 'where is Wither?'

'And you will all stop being mean to Wither,' the fortune teller went on, 'and you will allow him to recite poetry all day, and—'

Tabitha laughed, and Humphrey bumped into the table, and the crystal ball rolled onto the floor, and the fortune teller tumbled from her chair, the wig falling from her bald head.

37

'Wither!' Agatha said. 'Who'd have thought you'd look so delightful in a dress?'

Wither tore off the dress, revealing his ordinary clothing, folded his arms, and started to blub.

6
The Old Victorian Pier

'That was a rotten stunt, Wither,' Pamela said as the six of us floated up the rickety wooden steps to the pier.

'Wither didn't mean any harm,' I said, though only to stop him blubbing. I even put my arm around the bony fool. 'He was just getting into the holler-day spirit, weren't you, Wither?'

'That's right,' said Wither, wiping his eyes. 'The holler-day spirit, like Charlie said.'

'Well, we thought you were highly entertaining,' said Tabitha. 'Didn't we, Humphrey?'

Humphrey nodded, and gave his candyfloss a lick.

'Never mind all that,' I said, straightening my trilby. 'Look.'

The pier's ornate iron gates were secured with a chain, fastened with a heavy padlock. A sign hung across the bars read: FRIGHTEN PIER CLOSED UNTIL SPRING.

'We'll never get this thing off,' Humphrey said, examining the heavy padlock. 'Not without a skeleton key.'

'How are we meant to find poor Leslie if we can't get onto the pier?' said Tabitha.

'Perhaps there's a key hung on a hook on the other side,' I said. The bars were too close together to poke your head between them, so I doffed my trilby – the polite thing to do – and passed through the metal. 'No,' I said, passing back. 'Not a dickybird.'

'The key may be hidden from prying eyes,' said Pamela, and she wisped over the top of the gate to have a look.

We floated about for a minute or so, watching the seagulls squawk and flap, and then Wither wrinkled his brow. 'I have to say, Pamela is taking her time.'

A horrible thought occurred to me at that point. What if my mate Alfie Spectre hadn't wisped off down that alleyway last night? What if he'd been nabbed by that figure in the cape and top hat? And what if that same haunted heinousity had captured our Pammy?

Poor Pamela Fraidy, I thought as I peered between the bars. She's a nervous wreck as it is, and that caped figure is enough to give any ghosty a fright.

'She was probably distracted by the

41

attractions,' Agatha said. 'You know how flitty she is.'

'Yes,' I said nervously. 'She's just having a look around, that's all.'

'Charlie,' Tabitha said, 'you're shaking. Whatever is the matter?'

'It's this cold weather,' I said. I passed through the gate for a quick flit, and when I saw Pamela I breathed a sigh of relief. 'There she is, by the slot machines. And look, she's found the key. Wither, Humphrey, wisp over the gate and tell Pamela to float back and let us in.'

Wither and Humphrey frowned and wisped off.

Two minutes passed, and the ghosties did not return.

'It's getting dark,' I said. 'We need that key, or we'll be floating about out here all night.'

'Float after them, Aggie,' said Tabitha, and

43

Agatha adjusted her floppy sunhat and floated off, leaving just Tabitha and myself.

Two minutes passed, and Agatha did not return.

'I can see Humphrey,' Tabitha said a minute later. 'He's eating an I-scream.'

'I could pass through the gate,' I said, 'round up the four of them, grab the key from Pamela and flit back.'

'No need,' said Tabitha, and over the gate she wisped.

7

Hall of Mirrors

I decided I'd better tell the other ghosties about the caped figure. If I didn't, and that top-hatted horror nabbed me like it had nabbed Alfie Spectre, the other ghosties would never know what had happened.

Tabitha is the most sensible ghosty, so I approached her the moment I'd floated over the gate. 'Tabitha, there is something I have to tell you.'

'You can tell me when we're all together,' Tabitha said. 'Where did the other ghosties wisp off to? Let's try in here.' And she wisped beneath the door of this long wooden hut.

Along the side of the hut the words HALL OF MIRRORS were painted in huge white letters. I doffed my hat at the sign – an odd thing to do, perhaps, but a polite thing to do all the same – and passed through the wood.

'There's Pamela,' Tabitha said.

'Where?' I said, glancing at my reflection in one of the mirrors. The wobbly glass made my head look like a grape with a pencil-thin moustache.

'There,' Tabitha said, pointing.

I turned to where Pamela Fraidy was cowering in a corner by one of the mirrors, chewing her fingernails and quivering.

'Poor Pammy,' Tabitha said. 'These mirrors can give one quite a fright, and Pamela Fraidy is a nervous wreck as it is.'

As Tabitha and myself wisped to the rescue, I caught sight of a top hat reflected in one of the mirrors.

'Then we must escort her to safety,' I said, doffing my trilby at the caped figure's reflection. 'After all, it is the polite thing to do.'

I grabbed Tabitha and Pamela by the hand and wisped them under the door.

8
Bumper Cars

'Pamela,' Tabitha said as we flitted about outside, 'I need to have a word with Charlie. Would you mind awfully?'

I thought perhaps Tabitha had seen the caped figure in the Hall of Mirrors.

'Not at all,' Pamela said, and she folded her arms and turned the other way. 'One knows when one is not wanted.'

'You are wanted, Pammy,' Tabitha said. 'I just need to have a word with Charlie, that's all.'

'About what?' Pamela said, peering at

Tabitha over her shoulder. 'Nothing to worry about, I hope?'

'Not at all,' said Tabitha. 'I say, isn't that Humphrey on the Bumper Cars?'

We floated over the planks, waves crashing far below, to a brightly painted arena with the words BUMPER CARS painted across the front.

'It looks frightfully fun,' Tabitha said.

'I'd say it looks frightfully frightening,' Pamela said.

We watched for a bit, then Pamela said, 'Shouldn't he be sat at the wheel, rather than bumping the cars with his belly?'

'He'll be sick,' Tabitha said, 'bumping about after all that candyfloss and I-scream.'

I floated into the red car and Humphrey squeezed in beside me, and Tabitha and Agatha wisped into a green car with a dented bonnet.

'The electricity is switched off,' I said.

'Humphrey, you will have to get out and bump.'

'Tabitha,' Humphrey said, 'you could boot up the electricity using your skills.'

'What skills?' said Tabitha, shyly.

A moment later, however, the light bulbs hung around the top of the arena illuminated the night sky, red and yellow and blue and green, and this waltzy-schmaltzy music started up and the cars began to move.

Bump, bump, bump!

9
Ghost Train

When we got off the Bumper Cars, Pamela had turned as white as a, um, ghost, and Humphrey looked like he was about to be sick.

'I never knew bumping could be such fun,' Tabitha said, and she bumped into me, Pamela and Humphrey.

'This is no time for japes,' I said. 'We have to find the other ghosties before—'

Before the caped figure nabs them, I thought to myself, but I didn't say this out loud. I didn't want to frighten poor Pamela.

'Talking of finding the other ghosties,' Tabitha said, 'isn't that dear old Withaniel?'

Withaniel is Wither's full first name. Withaniel Scunthorpe the Third.

'Where?' I said. I could just make out the blue-black line where the sea met the sky, with the rides and amusements silhouetted against the night.

'It's difficult to see much in the dark,' Tabitha said. And she winked at me, and another string of bulbs lit up, and then another and another, until every bulb on Frighten Pier glowed a garish hue.

We floated over to a spookily painted building with cut-outs of skeletons and spectres nailed to the front, the words GHOST TRAIN painted across the top in luminous yellow paint.

'Wither,' Tabitha said, 'what are you doing?'

Wither looked up from where he was sat in one of the cars. 'The ghosties keep being mean to me. I'm going home.'

'I'm sure they didn't mean it, Wither.'

'Don't go home,' I said, doffing my trilby.

'We're on holler-day.'

'I need a holler-day from your meanness,' Wither said, and the wheels began to turn and the row of cars rolled along the track and in through a spookily painted wooden door.

'Your doing?' I asked Tabitha.

A minute later, this other spookily painted door opened and the row of cars rumbled out and came to a halt.

Wither frowned. 'I seem to have missed my stop.'

'This train won't take you home,' Tabitha said. 'The Ghost Train is a fairground ride. It's meant to be scary.'

'But it isn't scary at all,' Wither said. 'There's just a handful of jingly-jangly skeletons and so forth.'

'That doesn't mean it will take you home,' said Tabitha, and again the train of cars disappeared into the tunnel.

10
Ferris Wheel

After two more goes on the Ghost Train, Wither admitted defeat and floated out from the car. 'The only place that train takes you is back where you started.'

'We did try to explain,' Tabitha said kindly.

'I say, what happened to the other ghosties?' Wither said, glancing round.

'We're trying to round them up,' I said.

Wither looked at me like I'd gone mad. 'We?'

'Me and Tabitha,' I said. 'We've found Pammy and Humphrey, and—' But when I turned around, Tabitha, Pamela and Humphrey had gone. 'Now where might those three have wisped off to?'

'I'm in here, with Humphrey,' I heard Tabitha call. 'Though I don't know what happened to Pamela.'

Wither and myself followed Tabitha's floaty, ghostly voice further up the pier to a covered arcade. Flickering lights spelt the word AMUSEMENTS across the front. Inside, the arcade was lined with slot machines, one-armed bandits, that sort of thing.

'We'd better find the others,' I told Tabitha. 'There is something sinister going on, and—'

'Not yet,' Tabitha said. 'Humphrey and I are about to make our first million.'

Tabitha and Humphrey were floating above a carpet of coins that glistened silver and gold in the glare of the garish bulbs.

'What the devil are you doing?' Wither asked.

'Cheating,' Humphrey said, and he gave one of the machines an almighty bump with that big greedy belly. Several hundred coins

clattered to the floor.

Wither pulled a face like he was chewing a wasp. 'This is dishonest.'

'We won't keep a penny of it,' Tabitha said. 'We just wanted to feel rich for a moment, that's all. Come on, Humphrey. We must find the others.'

'Money isn't everything,' Humphrey said with a glum shrug. He gave the coins a wave

59

goodbye and followed Wither, Tabitha and myself out into the night.

Outside, we flitted about until I spotted Pamela and dear Aggie, screaming their haunted heads off at the top of the Ferris Wheel.

'Such high spirits,' Wither said as we looked up.

'Yes,' Tabitha said. 'They're enjoying themselves immensely.'

'We'll never find Leslie at this rate,' Wither said with a blub.

I was about to doff my trilby when I thought I saw something black circle against the night sky.

Tabitha fixed me with a serious gaze. 'Charlie, whatever is the matter? You've been on edge all afternoon.'

'Nothing,' I told her, and I straightened my tie.

'But there is something wrong, isn't there? You've seen something. I know because I've seen it too. A caped figure dressed in black.'

'You've seen it too?'

'What's all this about a caped figure?' Wither said.

I shrugged. 'Um, would you like to buy a wristwatch?'

11
The Old Victorian Music Hall

When we were all together, myself, Tabitha Tumbly, Wither, Humphrey Bump, Agatha Draft and a somewhat shaken Pamela Fraidy, we set off in search of Headless Leslie.

To Tabitha and myself, the matter had become urgent. We were the only two ghosties who knew about the caped figure in the top hat.

'We should split up, Charlie,' Wither said.

'Rubbish. It took us an hour to find each other.'

'Charlie is right,' Tabitha said. 'And I don't think any of us should be alone on a pier on a dark winter's evening.'

'There's a lot of funny people about,' I added, thinking back to when Alfie Spectre had used these exact words.

'Who knows what horrors may lurk,' Wither groaned.

'Shh,' Agatha said. 'You'll frighten Pamela.'

'What's all this talk of horrors?' Pamela asked Wither.

'It's nothing,' Tabitha told her, touching her quivering arm. 'Wither was reciting a poem. Weren't you, Wither?'

'If it's nothing,' Pamela said, 'why are you and Charlie so afraid? Tabitha, you and Charlie Vapour are the bravest ghosties I know. If this – this horror – is enough to unnerve the two of you, then it must be truly frightful.'

'Honest,' Tabitha said, 'it's nothing. Charlie and I have overactive imaginations.'

'Yes,' I said, straightening my trilby. 'The

mind plays tricks. Let's get on with our search.'

We flitted between the rides for a bit, but found no sign of Headless Leslie, not so much as a head.

'There is only one place left to look,' Wither said in his poetry voice. 'At the end of the pier, where the wind howls, the wood creaks and the seagulls fear to flap.'

Pamela wisped behind Tabitha and plugged her ears with her fingers.

'But where at the end of the pier?' Tabitha said.

Wither extended a bony finger, and pointed towards a rickety building with no windows and an angular wooden staircase leading up to a grand doorway. The sight of the wonky roof prompted me to straighten my trilby.

'Off you go then,' I told the cowardly old fool. 'We'll wait out here.'

'You won't catch me in there,' Wither said.

'What is that building anyway?'

'That,' Agatha said, 'is the Old Victorian Music Hall. It's a sort of musical theatre. There'll be rows of seats and a stage with a red velvet curtain.'

'Why didn't you say so?' said Wither. 'I love musical theatre.' And he floated off towards the building.

A moment later, he floated back.

'Wither,' Tabitha said, 'whatever is the matter?'

'I saw – a shadow.'

'There are a lot of shadows,' Agatha told Wither breezily. 'It's a dark winter's evening, and we're on a pier lit by fairground lights.'

No sooner had these words blown from Agatha's lips when the lights went out. Every

66

bulb on that pier fizzed and crackled and popped, leaving us poor ghosties with only the moon to light our way.

'Perhaps someone flipped the lever,' Tabitha said.

'Either that or it flipped itself,' said Humphrey, and Pamela hid behind the curve of his belly.

'I felt a spot of rain,' Agatha said, arching an elegant hand. 'Let's float inside.'

'What's that sound?' Wither cried, clamping a bony hand to his mouth. 'I heard a sound like – like souls escaping from a morgue.'

'It's just the wind,' Tabitha said.

'All perfectly innocent then,' said Wither. 'Just one point, however. A moment ago there were six of us. And now, quite suddenly, there are seven.'

'Rubbish,' I said. 'You miscounted.'

'Then who is that chap in the purple cape,

with eyes like burning coals and a tombstone top hat?'

'Ghosties,' I said, as the caped figure towered overhead, 'I think we had better wisp off.'

12

Trapped!

As we floated up the rickety old stairs of the Old Victorian Music Hall, the door swung open, which somehow felt both welcoming and terrifying at the same time, and we found ourselves in this vast candlelit space.

The door slammed behind us with a THUD.

'Bump it,' I told Humphrey, and he bumped and bumped and bumped, but the door would not open.

'The wood is too heavy,' Humphrey said, his hair standing on end, 'and the bolt is orange with rust.'

'That door is the only thing around here that isn't falling apart,' said Pamela Fraidy.

'You speak for yourself,' said Wither.

We wisped this way and that, 'henceforth and sideways,' as Wither put it, the daft old goat, until Agatha Draft rattled her pearls and declared that we were trapped.

'Trapped?' Wither said, gripping his jaw with his quill-like fingers.

'Trapped,' Agatha said.

The six of us floated about for a bit, then Wither said, 'So we're trapped then?'

'Trapped,' Agatha said, and she clutched her pearls to her chest.

'Trapped, trapped, trapped!' Wither cried, his poetry voice echoing around the hall. I told him to stop blubbing, and he turned to me and said, 'It's all right for you, Charlie Vapour. You can pass through. The rest of us are trapped, trapped, trapped!'

'Wither is right,' Tabitha said. 'Charlie, you can float off home whenever you like.'

'And leave my ghostly friends in Frighten with that caped figure?'

'But what a place to be trapped,' said Agatha. 'Tabitha, light the rest of those candles.'

'Turn away then,' Tabitha said, and we turned away. When we turned back, the Old Victorian Music Hall was lit by the warm glow of the hundreds of candles that lined the walls.

'I say,' Pamela said. 'What a charming interior.'

'It's like an old-fashioned cinema,' Humphrey

71

said, 'but without the screen.'

Wither shook his head. 'It's more like a church, but with comfy seats instead of pews.'

To me it looked like exactly what it was. A shabby old musical theatre, the sort that makes you want to take your hat off.

'Spook-tacular it may be,' Pamela said, 'but we still need to find the way out.'

'Perhaps Leslie knows the way out,' Tabitha said. 'We must find him. And I know how.'

Wither arched an eyebrow. Then, he arched the other eyebrow. 'Oh yes?'

'This musical theatre is the reason Headless Leslie floated to Frighten in the first place. There is nothing Leslie likes more than musical theatre.'

'You think Leslie might be trapped in here with us?' Pamela said.

'If he's not inside, he'll be somewhere close by.'

'But how do we find him?' Agatha said.

'Look around you,' said Tabitha. 'We have curtains, a stage, and row upon row of seats.'

'Explain,' I said, politely doffing my hat.

'We put on a show,' Tabitha said, 'and wait for Leslie to come to us.'

'What a splendid idea,' Wither said.

'Every ghosty loves a show,' said Agatha.

13
Headless Leslie

I went on first.

I grabbed this elegant cane from backstage, tipped my trilby and performed a dapper tap dance. Tabitha did her best to follow me with the spotlight. My shoes passed through the wood, so I made the tapping sound with a click of the tongue.

By the time I'd finished my second number, every seat in the Old Victorian Music Hall was occupied. Ghosties had wafted in from all over Frighten. How the ghosties got into the building I don't know, but judging by how see-through they were, I reckon they were the sort who ain't got much presence, if you know what I mean.

Next up was Agatha Draft, who blew a terrifying tune on the Old Victorian Pipe Organ. The audience found Agatha's tune terribly moving, so moving in fact that the front two rows blew away.

Then came Pamela's turn. She'd promised us a tune, but no sooner had she sung the first note than she got stage fright. Tabitha had to lower the curtain while Agatha led her from the stage.

I was hoping that would be the end of the show, but Wither insisted on reciting one of his poems. Funnily enough, it all worked out for the best.

Most theatres have a trapdoor in the centre of the stage, and this theatre was no different. The moment Wither cleared his throat, Humphrey Bump did the decent thing and bumped the lever that operates the trapdoor, and the trapdoor dropped open.

Now, ghosties can't stand on floorboards, as you know, but the trapdoor created a draft, and the draft sucked old Shakespeare through the square hole, and he vanished into the darkness.

'Humphrey, there was no call for that,' Agatha said.

'Oh, I don't know,' I said. 'Wither's poems are frightful.'

'I have to admit, you have a point,' Agatha said. 'But even so.'

'We'd better find him,' said Tabitha, wisping out from behind the curtain.

'Wait,' Pamela said. 'Look who's turned up.'

'Headless Leslie,' Tabitha said, and we all floated down to the front row, where Leslie was sat with his head in his lap, his fingers plugging the ears.

'Wither's poems are drivel,' Leslie said.

'I don't think we'll be hearing any more from Wither for a while,' I said.

The trapdoor had swung shut, and I was the only ghosty who had noticed. I should have mentioned this to Tabitha, but, well, I had to say hello to my old mate Leslie, and what with one thing and another—

Let's just say I forgot.

14

The Magician

'It looks like there's another act,' Leslie said, lifting his head onto his shoulders. Leslie wears this Elizabethan ruffle collar, so the head stays on a treat. It only falls off when he nods it, which explains why Leslie never agrees to anything.

We were all sat in the front row, the girls to Leslie's left, Humphrey and me to his right. Tabitha had closed the red velvet curtain, but now it began to twitch and sway, and as the curtain lifted, the spotlight settled on the bare wooden boards of the stage.

'There's no need for that,' I told Tabitha. 'We've all performed our party pieces, and

Leslie's turned up.'

'Most of the audience have faded away,' Humphrey said, glancing behind at the rows and rows of empty seats. 'Let's find the way out and float off home.'

'It wasn't me,' Tabitha said.

I gulped. 'If it wasn't you, then who—'

Pamela hid under her seat.

Then the organ started up, sort of whirly and swirly, and who should waft garlic-like onto the stage but the caped figure.

If I'd still had skin, I'd have leapt out of it.

'It's all right, Charlie,' Agatha said, clutching her pearls. 'He's a magician, and he's here to perform his breathtaking illusions. I read about him in a leaflet back at the hotel.'

'That explains the mantelpiece moustache and candlestick sideburns,' said Pamela, floating out from beneath her seat.

'But that's the ghosty who nabbed my mate

Alfie Spectre.'

'Agatha is right,' Tabitha said. 'That ghosty is an authentic Victorian conjuror. His name is The Great Conjuro.'

'What a splendid name,' I said, still shaken, I have to admit.

'If there is anything sinister going on,' Agatha said, 'we'll find out soon enough. Until then, I intend to sit back and enjoy the performance.'

So that was that. Nabbed mate or no nabbed mate, there was nothing for it but to settle in our velvet seats and watch the show.

And what a show it was!

First, he pulled this silk hanky from his pocket and stuffed it into his left hand, and when he opened his hand the hanky had vanished. He then pulled the hanky out of his sock and blew his nose.

Then, he produced an umbrella from behind

his elbow, and the umbrella turned into a bouquet of flowers and the flowers turned into a sword and the sword turned into a deck of playing cards and the cards turned into a bowl of smiling goldfish.

You should have heard our applause when The Great Conjuro vanished the bowl up his sleeve!

'For my grand finale,' the magician said in his booming cannonball voice, 'I will perform the greatest illusion in all magic.'

Agatha gasped.

'For this trick I require a volunteer from the audience,' The Great Conjuro said. Then he coughed into the back of his hand and added, 'One who doesn't mind having his head sawn off.'

'I volunteer,' Agatha said, raising a swan-like hand.

'I have to say,' Pamela said, 'you're terribly brave. I would volunteer myself, but the truth is, I'm afraid.'

'Pick me, pick me!' Agatha shrieked, but the magician grabbed Headless Leslie by the arm and wisped him onto the stage.

'That's not fair,' Agatha wept. 'Leslie didn't even volunteer.'

'I wonder why he chose Headless Leslie,'

I said, and the other ghosties shrugged.

'Perhaps Leslie's tunic looks good under the stage lights,' Pamela said.

The magician floated behind the curtain stage-left, then floated back, wheeling an ornate wooden box.

'Why does the box have eight wheels,' I said. 'Four would be enough, surely.'

'The box has eight wheels,' Agatha said, 'so that the magician can separate the box into two sections at the end of the trick. My father took me to magic shows all the time, when I was a little girl.'

'I don't know why he has to saw Leslie's head off,' Pamela said. 'Why not just shake him by the hand and bid him good day?'

'Shh,' said Agatha. 'The greatest illusion in all magic is about to begin.'

15
The Magician's Illusion

The moment Leslie lay back in the ornate wooden box, The Great Conjuro closed the lid.

With a flourish of his cape, the magician produced a saw from thin air, and the organ music stopped and this ghostly orchestra materialised in the orchestra pit. The magician sawed a notch in the wooden box, about a head's length from the end, and began to saw through the wood.

'I genuinely do not know how this trick is done,' said Agatha Draft.

'It's simple,' said Tabitha. 'You see—'

Agatha covered her ears with her hands. 'Don't tell me.'

'Leslie's head is detachable, as you know, and—'

'I don't want to hear this,' Agatha said.

The magician sawed and sawed and sawed, until the wooden box broke into two sections. We all gasped, then clapped our haunted hands.

'Incredible,' I said.

'Breathtaking,' said Tabitha Tumbly.

'Horrific,' cried Pamela Fraidy.

'Awesome,' grinned Humphrey Bump.

'I wish he'd saw Wither's head off,' Agatha said. 'I say, where is Wither?'

'He's still down that trapdoor,' I said. 'I suppose we'd better rescue him. If he has to find his own way out, we'll never hear the end of it.'

'I'm not going down there,' Pamela said. 'It's dark, and there'll be plankton.'

'I don't think any of us want to go down

there,' Agatha said. 'That's why it was so terribly mean of Humphrey to bump that lever.'

'Wither will be all right,' said Tabitha. 'He'll find a knot in the wood and wisp out into the night.'

'Shh,' Agatha said. 'We're missing the show.'

The Great Conjuro took a bow, then wheeled the head-sized end of the ornate wooden box away from the main section, and lifted it from the metal frame so that we could see Leslie's smiling head inside.

As the five of us floated up from our seats to applaud, the magician bowed so low that the head-end of the box tipped up and Leslie's head rolled out. The ghostly head did not stop rolling until it dropped through a gap in the boards at the back of the stage.

'The magician did that on purpose,' I said. 'I knew something was up, and this proves it.'

'Nonsense,' Agatha said.

89

The Great Conjuro bowed once more, and vanished in a puff of purple smoke.

Agatha frowned. 'Oh dear.'

'He's probably gone to fetch the head,' said Tabitha.

I removed my hat and scratched my bald patch. 'He's a magician, Tabitha. If he wanted the head back he'd conjure it up with his magic.'

'It isn't real magic,' Tabitha said.

'Oh, I'm quite sure it is real,' Agatha said breezily. 'At least, I like to think so.'

'It's all done with misdirection and sleight of hand,' Tabitha explained.

'And mirrors,' Pamela said. 'And lengths of cable with trumpets on the end.'

'I have to say,' Tabitha said, glancing down at her knees, 'I think Charlie might be right. Whether the magician uses real magic or skills, or, um, dangling trumpets, it's difficult to imagine such a talented ghosty dropping a head by mistake.'

'That's exactly what I thought,' I said, straightening my trilby.

'And if he had gone to fetch the head,' Tabitha said, 'wouldn't he be back by now?'

16
Velvet Trousers

Wither could find his own way out, but unless we rescued Leslie's head, it would spend several years rolling around in the dust – sneezing, due to Leslie's dust allergy – while the rest of him wandered in circles.

'It won't budge,' said Humphrey Bump. He was trying to shift the lever so that we could float down the trapdoor, but he kept bouncing off.

Us ghosties can wisp through a hole the size of a moth's nostril, and I can pass through, but it's preferable to have a bit of elbow room, if you know what I mean, and for breakfast that morning Humphrey had eaten twelve plates of chips.

Not only that, but the trapdoor would have let in some light.

'The magician must have jammed the lever,' Agatha said, 'using magic.'

'Or sleight of hand,' said Tabitha.

'There's nothing else for it,' Pamela said with a gulp. 'We will have to wisp into the darkness.'

'Let's not be hasty,' Tabitha said. 'There has to be another way down.'

'Tabitha,' I said after a quick nose around, 'I've found a door, and a staircase leading downwards.'

The trapdoor was situated in the centre of the stage, like I said, but the door was at the back, tucked away behind the curtain. I'd found the door by doffing my hat and passing through the curtain, and I knew there was a staircase behind the door because I'd passed through the wood.

'We could wisp under the door,' Pamela said, 'but that would be no better than wisping through a gap in the floorboards. Tabitha, you must use your skills.'

'All right,' Tabitha said, 'but do allow me a little privacy. You know how shy I am.'

Agatha, Pamela, Humphrey and myself faced the other way, and we heard this curtain-woosh sound and a clicky-clicky turning sound, and when we looked back, the curtain had been drawn to the side and the door swung on its hinges.

'Bravo, bravo,' Agatha said, clapping her ivory hands.

'Really,' Tabitha said, 'it was nothing.'

'I doubt this will take us below the stage,' Pamela said. 'The stairs lead off to the side.'

'It's worth a try,' said Tabitha. 'Show us the way, Charlie.'

'Um, ladies first,' I said, hiding behind my trilby.

'After you, Charlie Vapour,' Agatha said.

'I suppose it's up to me,' said Tabitha Tumbly, but just as she was about to wisp off, my hat toppled from my head and sailed down the staircase.

'Tabitha, you did that with your powers, so I'd have to float down and fetch it.'

'With my limited skills?' Tabitha said with a smile.

'You'd better fetch your hat,' Pamela said, 'before the magician nabs it.'

I adjusted my cufflinks and floated down into the darkness.

Then, I floated back up. 'My bald patch is cold,' I said, and Humphrey laughed.

'Get on with it,' Agatha said.

'Perhaps,' Pamela said, 'we should all float down together. It's less frightening that way.'

So the four of us joined hands and floated through the doorway and down the staircase, myself, then Tabitha, Pamela and Agatha, with Humphrey Bump bumping along at the rear, to the carpeted hallway at the bottom.

'It's not creepy at all,' said Pamela. 'Well, perhaps a little.'

The hallway was lined with seven doors, and one of the doors had been painted with a gold star.

'They're dressing rooms,' said Agatha. 'These are the rooms where the Victorian performers would rehearse their lines, apply make-up and prepare to tread the boards.'

'The room with the gold star will be the star's dressing room,' Tabitha said. 'Every show has a star, and the star would demand the grandest dressing room of all.'

'Then this,' I said, straightening my tie, 'is where we will find the magician.'

97

The moment I mouthed that final word, the door with the gold star creaked open, and an eerie purple light illuminated the dim hallway.

'Purple is The Great Conjuro's favourite colour,' said Agatha. 'I read that in a magazine.'

'Is he in there?' Pamela said, cowering behind Humphrey.

'I can't see anything with that purple light,' I said, but as I floated towards the dressing room door the light faded, and the interior of the dressing room wafted into view.

And there he sat, the mean-spirited magician in the purple cape and the black top hat.

'He's seen us,' I said, floating backwards. 'Perhaps we should wisp off.'

'But what about Leslie's head?' said Agatha. 'I say, where is Leslie?'

'The last time I saw him,' Pamela said, 'he was caught up in the stage curtain. I thought it best to leave him where he was.'

We all floated forwards and peered into the room. The Great Conjuro was sat on a chair, staring at his reflection in a mirror framed with bone-white light bulbs.

'I say,' Pamela said, 'the magician is awfully tall, even when seated.'

'I bet he's sitting on a plump cushion with tassels,' Agatha said. 'The Great Conjuro has frightfully good taste.'

'One way to find out,' I said. 'Agatha, waft the magician's cape with a ghostly draft.'

Agatha sighed. 'If only I had the required skill set.'

'This is no time for false modesty,' Tabitha said. 'The magician is sitting on something, and I think I can guess what it is.'

'Avert your gaze, then,' Agatha said.

We all closed our eyes – or pretended to – while Agatha rustled up an eerie breeze, and the magician's cape floated to one side and came to rest hooked over the back of the chair.

The Great Conjuro was not sat on a plump cushion with tassels as Agatha had thought. Wedged between the seat of the magician's velvet trousers and the chair was Leslie's head.

'Leslie!' I called in a loud whisper. 'Are you all right?'

'A tad squished,' Leslie said. 'Perhaps you could rescue me?'

Just as I was about to reply, The Great Conjuro fixed me with a magical gaze, tugging at the curve of his handlebar moustache.

We all floated back in horror, and tumbled about in the hallway.

'What a frightful predicament,' Agatha said. 'Poor Leslie.'

'I hope the magician is wearing clean underpants,' said Humphrey Bump.

17

Alfie Spectre

We were about to float back into the room when a door opened at the far end of the corridor. And who do you think floated out? None other than my old mate Alfie Spectre.

'Alfie! I thought you'd been nabbed.'

'I heard you had a spot of bother with The Great Conjuro,' Alfie said with a grin, 'so I floated over to see if I can help you out.'

I explained to Alfie that the magician had nabbed Leslie's head.

'The other week,' Alfie said, 'The Great Conjuro nabbed my mum's ghostly kitten.'

'What happened to the dear little thing?' Agatha asked, clutching her pearls.

'I gave the magician a gold ring, and he handed the kitten back unharmed.'

'Alfie buys and sells jewellery,' I explained. 'Watches, rings, that sort of thing.'

Tabitha coughed into the back of her hand. 'Where are your manners, Charlie?'

'Oh, right,' I said, straightening my tie. 'Alfie, these are my ghostly friends, Tabitha, Agatha, Pamela and Humphrey.'

'Charlie,' Tabitha said, 'perhaps you could give the magician a ring in exchange for Leslie's head.'

'That's the spirit,' Agatha said. 'There's always an answer if you put your heads together. No pun intended.'

'A ghostly head would cost you a lot more than a ring,' Alfie said. 'Unless the ring was highly valuable, of course.'

'I doubt we possess anything of high value,' Agatha said. 'Well, only my pearls—'

'And these,' I said, and I opened my jacket so the ghosties could see the half-dozen gold watches pinned to the lining. 'I bought these watches from Alfie during the night.'

Alfie scratched his head in thought. 'Charlie,' he said, 'those watches are exactly the sort of thing the magician would swap for a ghostly head.'

'How do you know so much about The Great Conjuro?' Humphrey asked, giving the boy a friendly bump.

'Oh, um. I must have read it somewhere.'

'Never mind that,' Leslie's head called out from the magician's dressing room. 'Just give the magician the watches and take me back to my body.'

To my relief, the moment I floated into the dressing room with my jacket open, The Great Conjuro smiled a twinkly, enigmatic smile and held out a white-gloved hand. I gave him the watches and flitted off.

'Charlie,' Tabitha said when I reached the doorway, 'I think you may have forgotten something.'

'You're right,' I said. 'It's nerves, see.'

Agatha rustled up a friendly breeze and blew me back into the dressing room.

'Erm, excuse me,' I said, holding my hat to my chest, 'I am sorry to trouble you, but I wonder if you will allow me the courtesy of – what I mean to say is – would you mind awfully—'

'Yes?' the magician boomed.

'Can we have our head back?'

'Certainly,' he replied, and immediately vanished in a puff of purple smoke.

So that was that. The Great Conjuro had wafted off, leaving us frightfully friendly ghosties to return the head to its rightful owner.

It wasn't until we floated up the stairs and

untangled poor Leslie from the curtains at the back of the stage, that we remembered poor Withaniel.

'We could have given the magician Wither's pocket watch,' Agatha said, holding the head in her elegant hands. 'That antique timepiece of his must be worth more than those six gold watches put together.'

'I say,' Agatha said, 'where is Wither?'

'He must still be down the trapdoor,' said Pamela.

Then we heard a muffled voice that seemed to come from the pocket of Alfie's army jacket. 'I never knew you were a ventriloquist, Alfie,' I said.

But Alfie looked as surprised as us lot.

'That sounded like Wither's voice,' Tabitha said. 'Alfie, I think you'd better unbutton your pocket.'

As Alfie unfastened the button, the flap flapped open and out wisped a certain Victorian poet.

'Wither,' Tabitha said, 'what were you doing in the pocket of Alfie's army jacket?'

'I didn't know it was Alfie's when I wisped into the pocket,' Wither said. 'The jacket was hung on a hook in one of the dressing rooms. I flitted into the pocket to hide from the magician.'

'Alfie likes to make himself at home,' I said with a wink. 'Ain't that right, Alfie?'

But Alfie just gazed down at his shoes.

'Alfred,' Wither said, 'it is time you returned Charlie's six gold watches.'

'I don't know what you're talking about,'

Alfie said, blushing a ghostly whitish red.

'You, Alfred,' Wither said, folding his bony arms, 'are a cheeky, lying rascal.' He pointed a wobbly finger at Alfie. 'This young man is in business with the magician. The Great Conjuro is nothing more than a great con artist.'

'Surely not,' Agatha gasped.

'Not only that, but Alfie here is his accomplice.'

Alfie held up his hands, protesting his innocence, but then he floated backwards and tripped over a heavy object caught up in the curtains. Tabitha parted the curtains using her skills, revealing an ornate wooden chest.

'Whatever is in that chest,' Alfie said, 'I don't know nothing about it.'

'Rubbish,' Wither said. 'I may be going deaf in my old age, but I could hear every word from that pocket.'

'What did you hear?' Tabitha asked him.

'Conversations between Alfred and the magician. It seems that the pesky pair have been working this scam for months.'

'And how does this scam work, Wither?'

'Well—'

'Wither,' I said, 'I think we should hear this from Alfie.'

'All right,' Alfie said. 'I'll come clean.'

And we gathered round and listened to what Alfie Spectre had to say.

'I sell the victim an item of value. Then, The Great Conjuro kidnaps a friend of theirs, and I tell the victim that the only way to save their friend is to offer the magician something of value in exchange.'

'And the victim gives the magician whatever it was you sold them,' Tabitha said.

Alfie grinned. 'I get to keep the goods and the victim's money.'

'That sounds like a lot of work,' I said. 'Most

criminals simply pick the victim's pockets, or break into their home and steal their ghostly television.'

'I'd end up in prison for that,' Alfie said. 'With this scam, the police would think I've done nothing wrong. It's the magician who does the nabbing, and no ghostly police force can arrest a magician.'

'The moment The Great Conjuro hears the jangle of handcuffs,' Agatha cried, clapping her hands, 'he will vanish in a puff of purple smoke!'

'Alfie,' Pamela said, 'what you and the magician have done is wrong. You didn't just steal Charlie's money. You stole our ghostly holler-day.'

'I was worried about you, Alfie,' I said. 'I really thought you'd been nabbed.'

'One further question,' Tabitha said to Alfie Spectre. 'You've told us what you get out of this con trick. But what's in it for The Great Conjuro?'

'I guess he just likes nabbing people,' Alfie said, and he wisped off.

'You should flit after him,' Humphrey said.

'He'll be on the other side of the pier by now,' I said, tidying my trilby. 'Alfie can out-wisp the best of them.'

'Thanks awfully,' Leslie's head said as Agatha returned it to Leslie's shoulders.

'Let's find the way out,' I said, 'and float off home.'

'Aren't we forgetting something?' Wither said. He floated towards the chest, flexed his bony fingers and opened the ornate wooden lid.

The chest was filled to the brim with watches, necklaces, bracelets and rings.

'We must return these items to their rightful owners,' Tabitha said.

'You will do no such thing,' a cannonball

voice boomed, and we all flitted round.

There, floating above the orchestra pit, was that great con artist The Great Conjuro, with Alfie Spectre tucked beneath one arm.

'We thought we'd seen the last of you, Alfie,' I said.

'Me and Cedric have had a chat,' Alfie said.

'Cedric is my real name,' the magician explained. 'The Great Conjuro is a stage name.'

'We'd never have guessed,' smirked Humphrey Bump.

'The boy Alfie has made me see sense,' Cedric said. 'What Alfred and I have done is wrong, and, much as I enjoy the odd nab, we intend to mend our ways and return the valuable items to their owners.'

'We'd like to help,' Agatha said, and she fluttered her elegant eyelashes. 'That is, if you wouldn't mind.'

'Don't worry,' Alfie said, 'we're not going to

wisp off and keep the items for ourselves.'

'Oh, we do believe you,' Tabitha said, 'but we really would like to help, wouldn't we, ghosties?'

'How frightfully friendly,' the magician said, and he beamed a magnificent smile.

AN INTERVIEW WITH DAREN KING

Who is your favourite ghostie?

Charlie Vapour. Like me, he's dapper and he looks good in a trilby.

Where do you normally write your stories?

At the funfair, on the rollercoaster. When it's raining I write at home.

What is your favourite colour?

Orange. No, blue. Wait . . . no, red. Definitely red.

Are you scared of the dark?

I find darkness comforting. It's like a warm, soft duvet.

Have you ever seen a ghost?

I've seen hundreds of ghosts, and all were frightfully friendly.

Where do you get your ideas from?

Most of my ideas come from conversations. If you talk about fun things with your friends, you will have fun ideas.

What is the worst job you've ever had?

I used to work as a secret agent. I was terrible at it. The problem was, I just can't keep a secret.

AN INTERVIEW WITH DAVID ROBERTS

Who is your favourite ghostie?

My favourite ghostie to draw is Rusty Chains because of his clanking chains and his miserable face.

Where do you normally write your stories?

I have always loved drawing. When I was very small my favourite things to draw were ladies wearing big dresses.

What is your favourite colour?

My favourite colour is grey because there are so many different shades. My second favourite colour is yellow.

Are you scared of the dark?

I thought I wasn't scared of the dark until last year in the Welsh countryside; there were no street lights and I had to walk through woods to get to my holiday cottage. It was so dark I could not even see my feet. There were creepy sounds all around me and I was TERRIFIED.

Have you ever seen a ghost?

No. I am very pleased to say that I haven't!

Win a family trip to Alton Towers

To win a fabulous day out at Alton Towers for you and your family plus spending money, pick your favourite ghostie from *Ghostly Holler-Day* and write a holiday postcard to him. Send us your entry on a plain piece of paper in no more than 100 words. You can also draw your ghostie on the paper if you like!

Visit www.frightfullyfriendlyghosties.co.uk for full terms and conditions.

Closing date: 31 December 2010